Narcissus and Echo

Welcome to the World of Mythology

Mythology gives interesting explanations about many tribulations in life and tries to satisfy your curiosity. Many stories have been created to explain surprising or frightening phenomena. Thus, different countries and peoples throughout the world have their own myths.

Greek and Roman mythology is deeply loved, because it is a treasury of imagination that weaves together the exciting legends of surreal gods, heroines, and heroes. As a mirror that reflects the human world, Greek and Roman mythology is recommended as a must-read in order to understand western culture and thinking.

Although the basis of these classical stories can be traced back as far as the prehistoric age, what is it in these myths that can still enchant you, a citizen of the contemporary world? The secret is that mythology transcends time and space and keeps intact the internal desires of human beings. The exciting adventures allow you unlimited access to the important aspects of life: war and peace, life and death, good and evil, and love and hatred.

The Olympian gods who appear in Greek and Roman mythology are not always described as perfect, omnipotent gods. As these gods fight in anger, trick other gods, and suffer the pain of love and jealousy, they often resemble humans. In Let's Enjoy Mythology, the second volume in the series Reading Greek and Roman Mythology in English, you can encounter many heroes, heroines, gods, and goddesses with very human characteristics.

Reading Greek and Roman Mythology in English will guide you through your journey into the imaginary world of the ancient Greeks. Your trip will be to a place that transcends time and space.

The characters in the stories

Narcissus

The beauty of Narcissus was compared to that of Adonis and Dionysus. He fell in love with his own reflection on a pool so much that he would not leave the pool. Pining away for love of himself, he died. The word, narcissism (self-admiration) originated from this myth.

Echo

In Greek mythology, Echo was the nymph of the woodlands and springs. Her name has a meaning of an echo. Owing to Hera's curse, Echo could repeat only the words of others. She fell in love with a very handsome young man, Narcissus. However, her love was rejected. In grief, Echo faded away, with her body turned into a stone, with the exception of her voice, echoing in the mountains.

Nemesis

She was the daughter of Nyx, the goddess of night. Nemesis was the goddess of righteousness and retribution. She is usually depicted as either carrying an apple-bough in one hand and a wheel in the other or driving in a chariot drawn by monsters.

Aphrodite

She was the goddess of beauty and the mother of Eros, the god of love. Aphrodite helped Adonis' mother, Smyrna, to turn into a tree, and gave Adonis to Persephone to raise him. Aphrodite fell in love with Adonis when he became an adult.

Adonis

In Greek mythology, Adonis was the son of King Cinyras of Cyprus and the king's daughter Smyrna. He escaped death with the help of Aphrodite. He was sent to the Underworld to be taken care of by Persephone. However, later he became Aphrodite's lover. Adonis was killed by the god of war, Ares. When he died, a flower called anemone sprung from his blood.

Cinyras and Smyrna

In Greek mythology, Cinyras was the king of Cyprus, and Smyrna was his daughter. Aphrodite cursed Smyrna to fall in love with her father, King Cinyras. Adonis was the son of Cinyras and Smyrna.

Before Reading *Narcissus and Echo*

This book contains the sad love stories of Narcissus and Echo and of Aphrodite and Adonis.

Story One

Echo was a beautiful nymph of the woods and springs, and she had a very attractive voice. However, she had one failing; she was fond of talking too much. Echo, by her talk, helped Zeus who was amusing himself among the nymphs. Enraged at Echo, Hera cursed her to speak only the words of others. One day, Echo saw a beautiful youth, Narcissus. Narcissus was beautiful but arrogant. He cruelly rejected Echo's love and hurt other nymphs.

Nemesis, the goddess of righteous vengeance, punished Narcissus for his cruel rejection. She made him fall in love with his own reflection in the water of a spring. His love for his image reflected on the surface of the water couldn't be consummated, as even with a finger's touch, his reflection would just disappear.

Story Two

King Cinyras bragged that his daughter Smyrna was as beautiful as Aphrodite, the goddess of beauty and love. The goddess was enraged and cursed Smyrna to fall in love with her father, King Cinyras. Disguising her true appearance, she slept with her father and gave birth to Adonis.

When Smyrna's father, King Cinyras realized what had happened, he couldn't forgive his daughter and tried to kill her. However, Aphrodite helped her turn into a tree. This is where the love story of Aphrodite and Adonis begins.

Let's read in detail about the love stories of Narcissus and Echo and of Aphrodite and Adonis.

Contents

Narcissus and Echo

01

Nymphs are beautiful female spirits of nature.
They spend their time playing or singing.
They do not live in houses or have cities.
They live in the wild. Nymphs who live in rivers and oceans are called water nymphs.
There are also tree nymphs and mountain nymphs.

This story is about a beautiful mountain nymph and a very handsome man.

A Day of Nymphs

Echo was the most charming
mountain nymph.
She was very beautiful and also
musically talented.
She could sing and play many
instruments.
Echo wanted to remain pure.
She promised herself that
she would never fall in love.

However, Echo had one fault.
She talked too much.
Some people found this amusing,
but some did not.
It was very difficult to argue with Echo.
She always got the last word.

One day, Zeus was playing with many
mountain nymphs.
Zeus often spent a lot of time with nymphs.
This made his wife, Hera, jealous.
Hera suddenly appeared near the top of
the mountain. She was angry.
Zeus, being a god, could sense that Hera
was near. He asked Echo to talk to Hera so
that everyone could escape.

02 As Hera came down the mountain, Echo greeted her.

"Where is my husband?" Hera asked.

"Oh, Hera, goddess of marriage and birth. You must know that Zeus is very lucky that you are his wife."

Echo's voice was very beautiful.

"But I have not seen Zeus," said Echo.
"I was just walking in the woods.
There are many beautiful flowers.
Look at this one!"
Hera listened to Echo for a few minutes.
That was enough for Zeus and the other
nymphs to get away.

But then Hera realized that Echo was lying. She was very angry with Echo.

"So you think you are clever," Hera told Echo. "Very well. You will lose the power to talk first. From now on, you will only be able to reply. You always like to have the last word. So be it! That is all you will have!"

And it was so.
Soon,
Echo discovered how
Hera punished her.
Echo was only able to
repeat what her
friends said.
And she was only
able to repeat the last
few words.

03

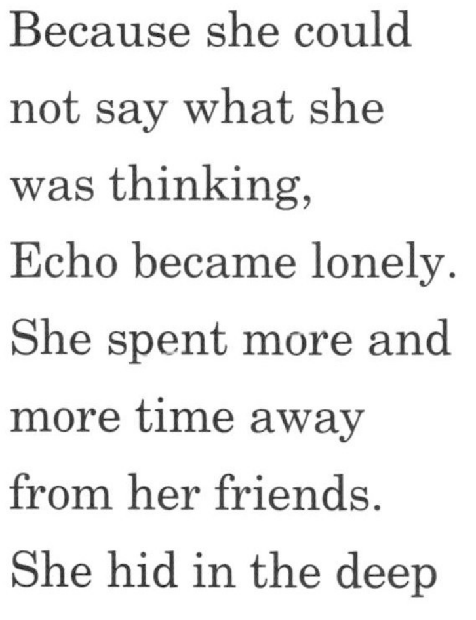

Because she could
not say what she
was thinking,
Echo became lonely.
She spent more and
more time away
from her friends.
She hid in the deep
woods.

There was a beautiful young man named Narcissus. Narcissus was the son of the river god, Cephisus and the nymph, Liriope.

When he was born, an oracle saw the baby's future. The oracle said, "Narcissus will live long if he never sees himself."

No one could figure out exactly what that meant.

But his mother was worried.

She would not permit her son to come near any mirrors.

She kept all shiny things away from him.

As a boy, Narcissus never saw his own face.

Narcissus was one of the most handsome
men in Greek history. His beauty was
compared to that of Adonis and Dionysus.
But Narcissus had a cold heart.
Many women and nymphs fell in love with
him. He rejected all of them.

04 One sunny afternoon, Narcissus was hunting
with his friends in the mountains.
They saw a deer and ran after it.
But Narcissus fell down.
When he got up, he couldn't see his friends.
He wandered up and down the mountain,
looking for them.
That's when Echo saw him.

Echo forgot her promise to remain pure.
Because she was lonely, and because
Narcissus was so handsome, Echo fell in love.
Echo followed after Narcissus as he wandered
around the mountain.
She hid in the shadows of the trees.

How she wanted to call out to him!
If only she could speak first!
He would fall in love with her voice.
But because of Hera,
Echo could not speak first.

After a while, Narcissus felt that someone was following him.
"Who's here?" he called out.
"Here!" cried Echo, desperately.
Narcissus looked around but he could see no one. "Come!" he called.
Echo immediately replied, "Come!"
Narcissus waited, but no one came.

He was confused so he called out again.
"Why don't you come to me?"
"Come to me!" cried Echo.
"Show me yourself," said Narcissus.
Echo repeated his words,
"Show me yourself!"

05 Echo ran out from behind the tree.
She tried to hug him.
Narcissus stepped back.
Echo was beautiful,
but Narcissus was proud.
"Keep your hands off me!" he shouted.
"I would rather die than let you have me!"
"Have me!" Echo pleaded.

But Narcissus's heart
was as cold as stone.
He had no pity for
Echo.
Narcissus walked
away from Echo
because he did not
like her.

After a few minutes,
Echo heard him
again calling out
for his friends.
But this time,
she did not reply.
She was ashamed.
She ran away,
crying.

Echo Turning Into a Rock

The other mountain nymphs never saw
Echo again.
Echo hid away in caves and mountaintops.
She avoided all contact with other nymphs.
She did not eat or drink.

Nymphs live a long, long time.
But they are not immortal.
Even they need food and water.

Soon Echo's body became thinner and
thinner.
Her flesh and muscles all shrunk.
She was nothing but skin and bones.
Then even her bones turned into rocks.
Nothing was left of Echo except her voice.

06 Hera had promised that Echo would always have the last word. And so Echo does.
Her voice can be heard near tall mountains.
It can be heard in deep caves.
You can hear it when you are hiking.
Just call out, and she will answer you.
Sometimes she will repeat your words twice or even three times.
If you are alone, Echo's voice may cheer you up. Or it might scare you.

Echo was not the last to fall in love with Narcissus. Many of her friends also fell in love when they saw the handsome young man.

But Narcissus did not like any of them.

'None of these nymphs are attractive to me,' he thought.

'I will not waste my love on any of them.'

One day, a nymph became angry at Narcissus.
She thought he was too proud of himself.
She loved him. But he rejected her.
So this nymph prayed to the gods.
"Narcissus needs to be punished," she prayed.
"He has no love for others.
Because of him, Echo suffered.
So let Narcissus love himself. Make him love himself as much as Echo loved him.
But do not let him have what he wants."

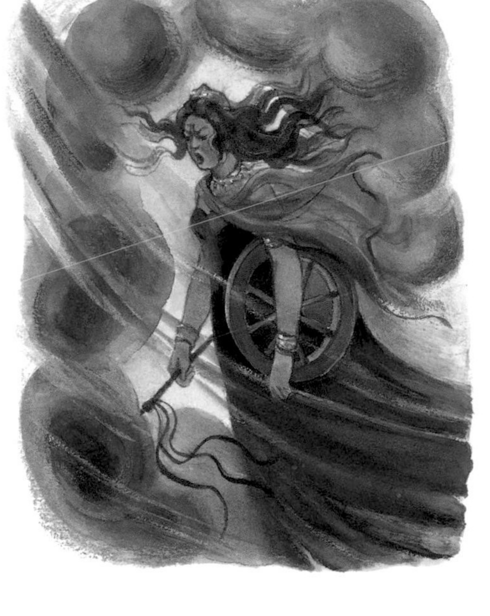

The goddess
Nemesis heard
the nymph's
prayers.
She was the
goddess of
justice and
vengeance.
Nemesis would
punish people
who hurt others.
She knew how Narcissus was mean to Echo.
She felt pity for Echo.
Nemesis saw how Narcissus treated the
other nymphs and young women.
She decided to answer the prayers of the
young nymph.
She would punish Narcissus for being so
mean and proud!

07 There was a hidden spring in the mountains where Narcissus hunted.

It was a beautiful and secret place.

No animal or human feet had walked on the grass around the water.

The water was like silver.

The grass around it was fresh, long, and green. Tall rocks protected the spring from the sun's rays.

It was a relaxing and magical place.

One day, Narcissus
was hunting as usual.
He was chasing a big
boar. But the boar was
fast. It ran through
thick bushes. It was
difficult for Narcissus
to follow the boar.

Soon, Narcissus became lost.
He tried to go back,
but he couldn't
remember the way.
He fell through some
bushes into a clear
space.
He had found the
hidden spring!

He felt lucky, because he was thirsty.
He knelt down to drink the water.
Suddenly, for the first time in his life,
he saw himself.
He froze and looked in amazement.

Narcissus saw a very handsome young man.
He had bright eyes and light brown hair.
His hair was curly like that of Dionysus or
Apollo. His cheeks were round and pale red.
His neck was like ivory, perfectly shaped.
The man's red lips were slightly open.
The young man looked very healthy.

08

Narcissus watched this image and fell in love with it. Never had he seen a face so beautiful. 'It must be a water spirit looking at me,' he thought.
He reached down to kiss those lips. But when he touched the water, the face disappeared!

Narcissus was alarmed and confused.
But soon he saw the face come back. He reached down to touch it.
Again, it disappeared.
And then it came back again.

He forgot his thirst and his hunger.
He looked at the image for a long time.
Then he dared to speak.
“Beautiful spirit, why do you run from me?
You must find me attractive.
The mountain nymphs all love me.”
But the image was silent.

Narcissus started to cry. His tears fell into the water. The image began to disappear.
"Please stay!" pleaded Narcissus.
"At least let me look at you. I promise I will not try to touch you again."
Narcissus remained still. He didn't move. He didn't even dare to blink.

Narcissus and Echo

For days, he sat and stared at the image.
And the image looked back at him.
Slowly, he lost the color in his face.
His health slowly went away.
The muscles on his long legs, slender arms,
and perfect neck became smaller.
He became weaker and weaker.
Soon he could not move. He could only look
at the image in the water.
He saw it also slowly changing.

Echo's spirit found him in this place.
She guessed what happened. She felt sorry for Narcissus. She still loved him.
But she could do nothing for Narcissus.
When he finally died, he made a small sigh.
Echo could only repeat it.

09 The other mountain nymphs soon found Narcissus's body. Even though he had rejected them, they wept over his death.
They prepared a funeral for him.

But when they came back, they could not find the body.
Instead they found a beautiful flower there. It had white petals and a purple middle.
The nymphs were amazed and sad.

They called this flower 'Narcissus' to remember him.

It is said that Narcissus still looks at his reflection in the underworld.
He is doomed forever to look at himself in the river Styx.

Aphrodite and Adonis

10 In the land of Cyprus,
there was a king named Cinyras.
He had two children,
a daughter named Smyrna
and a son named Adonis.
But Smyrna and Adonis were not
sister and brother.
This is the story of Adonis's
birth and death.

Before Adonis was born, Smyrna became a young woman. She was very beautiful! Cinyras was very proud of his daughter's beauty. He told everyone that his daughter looked like a goddess. He even said Smyrna was as beautiful as the goddess Aphrodite. Aphrodite was very beautiful, but she could also be very jealous. She did not like to be compared to a mortal girl.

Aphrodite decided to punish King Cinyras.

Aphrodite told her son Eros to shoot an arrow into Smyrna.

Eros's arrows were magical. His golden arrows caused people to fall in love with the first person they saw.

Aphrodite wanted Smyrna to fall in love with her father. So Aphrodite told her son to make this happen.

Eros waited until Smyrna was walking to see her father.
He shot one of his arrows into her heart.
Because it was magical,
Smyrna did not see it.
When Smyrna saw her father,
she fell in love with him.

11

Of course, it was
against the law to
love a relative.
People thought it
was a terrible thing
to do.
Smyrna knew it
was wrong.
But she could not
help herself.
The magic in Eros's arrow was too strong.

Smyrna tried to
kill herself.
But her nurse
found Smyrna
and stopped her.
The nurse
promised to help
Smyrna.

One day, Smyrna's mother left the city.
The nurse gave King Cinyras a lot of wine.
She told the king about a young woman
who truly loved him.
Then the nurse brought Smyrna to her
father's bedroom.
Because of the wine and the dark, the king
did not recognize his own daughter.
This continued for several nights.

One night, King Cinyras became curious.
He wanted to see this young woman's face.
So he didn't drink much wine.
After Smyrna came to him, he lit a candle.
When he saw his daughter's face, he became very angry. Smyrna ran out of the palace.
He grabbed a sword and chased after his daughter.

Smyrna ran into the forest, crying.
She prayed to the gods to make her invisible.
Aphrodite heard her, and decided to help.
Aphrodite turned Smyrna into a tree.
King Cinyras was right behind his
daughter. He saw her change into a tree.
He was still very angry.

He hit the tree very hard with his sword!
The tree split down the middle.
In the middle of the broken tree lay the baby Adonis.
He was the son of King Cinyras and Smyrna.

The tree did not die, however. It lived, and many other trees grew from its seeds.
Much later, people made perfume from this type of tree.

King Cinyras saw the baby Adonis.
He knew it was terrible to have a baby with his daughter.
He raised the sword again to kill Adonis.
But Aphrodite came down from heaven.
She grabbed Adonis and saved him.

Aphrodite put Adonis in a chest.
Then she took him to Persephone.
Persephone was the goddess of the underworld.
Aphrodite asked Persephone to take care of Adonis.

Persephone did her job well.

Adonis grew into a tall and strong young man.

Because his mother was so beautiful, Adonis became very handsome.

Many spirits in the underworld fell in love with Adonis. His beauty attracted even Persephone.

But Adonis was not interested. He didn't love anyone until he met Aphrodite again.

 13 It happened this way.

Aphrodite was playing with Eros.
Accidentally, she wounded herself with one of Eros's arrows. She pushed Eros away but the arrow's wound was deep.
Before it healed, she saw Adonis.
Aphrodite was immediately attracted to his beauty.

She wanted Adonis to live with her.
But Persephone would not let Adonis go.
Finally, the goddesses asked Zeus to solve their problem. Zeus did not want to get involved in this argument.
Instead, he sent the Muse, Calliope, to decide the matter.
Calliope tried to please both goddesses.

She told Adonis to spend one third of the year with Persephone. Then he would spend the next one third of the year with Aphrodite. For the last one third of the year, Adonis could choose his partner. Adonis always chose to be with Aphrodite for the last one third of the year.

Even so, Aphrodite wasn't completely pleased. She was jealous of Persephone for having just one third of the year with Adonis.

For two thirds of the year, Aphrodite spent all her time with Adonis.

Aphrodite and Adonis

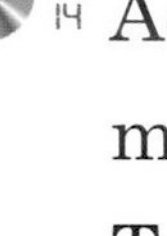

14 Adonis was a strong, adventurous young man. He loved to hunt wild animals. To be with him, Aphrodite would leave her heavenly home. Adonis was more precious to her than heaven. Aphrodite would change her lifestyle for him.

In heaven, Aphrodite would just lay in the shade. But with Adonis,
she would go hunting.
In heaven, Aphrodite would wear beautiful dresses. But with Adonis,
she would wear men's hunting clothes.
Aphrodite did not like the outdoors.
But for Adonis, she would run over hills and through the woods.
Aphrodite was the goddess of beauty.
But when she was with Adonis, she was more like Artemis, goddess of the hunt.

But Aphrodite was not bold.
She only hunted rabbits and deer with Adonis.
Aphrodite warned Adonis about hunting dangerous animals.
She told him not to hunt lions or boars.
"Be brave against the shy animals," she told Adonis.
"It is not safe to hunt the fierce beasts.
Be careful. Don't attack the animals that Nature has given weapons. Do not put yourself and our happiness in danger."
Aphrodite said .

"I will not love you more if you prove your bravery. Your beauty will not impress lions or boars.
Think of their terrible claws and teeth.
I hate those animals!"
After giving Adonis this warning,
Aphrodite prepared to leave.
She had an appointment on Cyprus.
She got into her chariot, which was pulled by magical swans. She drove away through the air.

15 But Adonis was too proud to follow Aphrodite's advice.

He was not a scared, weak boy. He was young and strong. So when his dogs found a boar in the bushes, Adonis chased after it. He threw his spear, and it stuck in the boar's side. But this wound was not serious.

The boar grabbed it with its mouth and pulled the spear out.

Some say this boar was actually Ares, the god of war. Ares was Aphrodite's lover before Adonis.
When Adonis was with Persephone, Ares would be with Aphrodite.
Ares was jealous of Adonis.
Some say that he changed himself into a boar.
In this way, he could kill Adonis secretly.

The boar ran at Adonis, and the young man ran for his life. But not many humans can run faster than a boar.
The animal caught up to Adonis and knocked him over.
Then the boar turned and buried its tusks into Adonis's stomach.

Adonis lay dying on the grass.
Finally, Adonis's dog chased the boar away.
But it was too late. He moaned out loud.

His cries were so loud that Aphrodite heard them. She turned her swan-driven chariot around and rushed back.

Adonis's Death

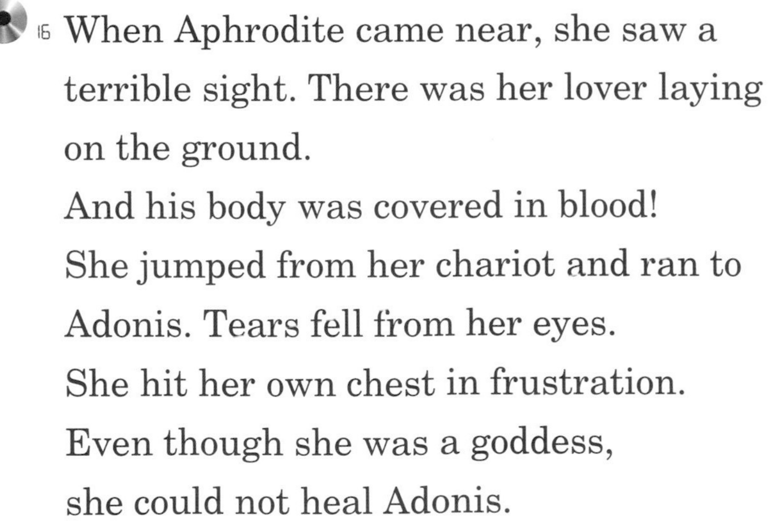

16 When Aphrodite came near, she saw a terrible sight. There was her lover laying on the ground.

And his body was covered in blood!

She jumped from her chariot and ran to Adonis. Tears fell from her eyes.

She hit her own chest in frustration.

Even though she was a goddess, she could not heal Adonis.

She grabbed her hair and pulled and shouted up at the sky.

"Oh, terrible fate, why do you treat me so? But this will not be a complete victory for fate. The memory of my grief will live on forever.

It will be made new every year.

My lover, Adonis, your blood shall be changed into a flower.

This flower will bloom every year to remind everyone of my love for you."

As she said this, Aphrodite poured some drops of 'nectar' on Adonis's blood. As the nectar and blood mixed, bubbles were formed.

After about an hour, a flower magically grew up.
It was dark red, like Adonis's blood. But this flower lives only a short time.
The wind blows the flower open quickly.
And then the wind blows the petals away.

For this reason, the flower is called 'Anemone', or 'Windflower'.
The wind helps the flower bloom, but it also destroys it.

Reading Comprehension

Read and answer the questions.

Narcissus and Echo

1. Why did Hera get mad at Echo?

   (A) Because Echo was Zeus's lover.
   (B) Because Echo lied to Hera.
   (C) Because Echo didn't want to fall in love.
   (D) Because Hera was jealous of Echo's voice.

2. What did Hera do to Echo?

   (A) She made Echo disappear.
   (B) She took away Echo's ability to speak first.
   (C) She made Echo fall in love.
   (D) She turned Echo into a boar.

3. What did the oracle say about Narcissus?

   (A) He will be the handsomest man in Greek.
   (B) He will not love anyone.
   (C) He will live long if he never sees himself.
   (D) He will hunt all his life.

4. Why did so many women and nymphs fall in love with Narcissus?
   (A) Because he was young and brave.
   (B) Because he could sing very well.
   (C) Because he was very handsome.
   (D) Because he was very proud.

5. What did Narcissus think of the women who fell in love with him?
   (A) He didn't like any of them.
   (B) He was afraid of all of them.
   (C) He loved all of them.
   (D) He didn't trust any of them..

6. What was Narcissus hunting when he became lost?
   (A) a deer
   (B) a rabbit
   (C) a bear
   (D) a boar

7. What did Narcissus find when he fell through the bushes?
   (A) a mirror
   (B) a shiny rock
   (C) a hidden spring
   (D) Echo

8. Who did Narcissus think his reflection was?
   (A) himself
   (B) a water spirit
   (C) a god
   (D) a nymph

9. What did the nymphs find when they returned for Narcissus's body?
   (A) a flower
   (B) just grass
   (C) blood
   (D) bones

10. Who was the god or goddess that punished Narcissus?

    ____

Aphrodite and Adonis

1. What relation was Smyrna to Adonis?
   (A) his sister
   (B) his mother
   (C) his aunt
   (D) his nurse

2. How did Aphrodite punish Cinyras?
   (A) She made Smyrna kill Cinyras.
   (B) She made Eros shoot a magical arrow into Cinyras.
   (C) She made Smyrna fall in love with her father, Cinyras.
   (D) She sent Ares to kill Cinyras.

3. How was Adonis born?
   (A) when a tree was split open
   (B) from his father's thought
   (C) a natural birth
   (D) from a wild animal

4. Who saved Adonis from his father?

(A) Persephone
(B) Smyrna
(C) the nurse
(D) Aphrodite

5. Where did Adonis grow up?

(A) in his father's palace
(B) in a cave
(C) in the underworld
(D) in Aphrodite's home

6. Why did Aphrodite fall in love with Adonis?

(A) She hurt herself with her son's magic arrows.
(B) She drank the wrong magical potion.
(C) She saw Adonis's beauty.
(D) She was jealous of Persephone.

7. How much of the year did Adonis spend with Persephone?

(A) one half
(B) two thirds
(C) four months
(D) three months

8. What did Ares feel towards Adonis?

(A) admiration
(B) jealousy
(C) love
(D) fear

9. How did Adonis die?

(A) He fell on his own spear.
(B) His own dog attacked him.
(C) A boar killed him.
(D) He fell from Aphrodite's chariot.

10. How did Adonis become a flower?

____

____

Read and talk about it.

. . . One day, a nymph became angry at Narcissus.
She thought he was too proud of himself.
She loved him. But he rejected her.
So this nymph prayed to the gods.
“Narcissus needs to be punished,” she prayed.
“He has no love for others.
Because of him, Echo suffered.
So let Narcissus love himself.
Make him love himself as much as Echo loved him.
But do not let him have what he wants.” . . .

1. How would you want Narcissus to be punished, if you were that nymph?

. . . She wanted Adonis to live with her. But Persephone would not let Adonis go.
Finally, the goddesses asked Zeus to solve their problem. Zeus did not want to get involved in this argument. Instead, he sent the Muse, Calliope, to decide the matter. Calliope tried to please both goddesses. She told Adonis to spend one third of the year with Persephone. Then he would spend the next one third of the year with Aphrodite. For the last one third of the year, Adonis could choose his partner.
Adonis always chose to be with Aphrodite for the last one third of the year. . . .

2. What would you have decided, if you were Calliope?

____

____

____

The Signs of the Zodiac

17

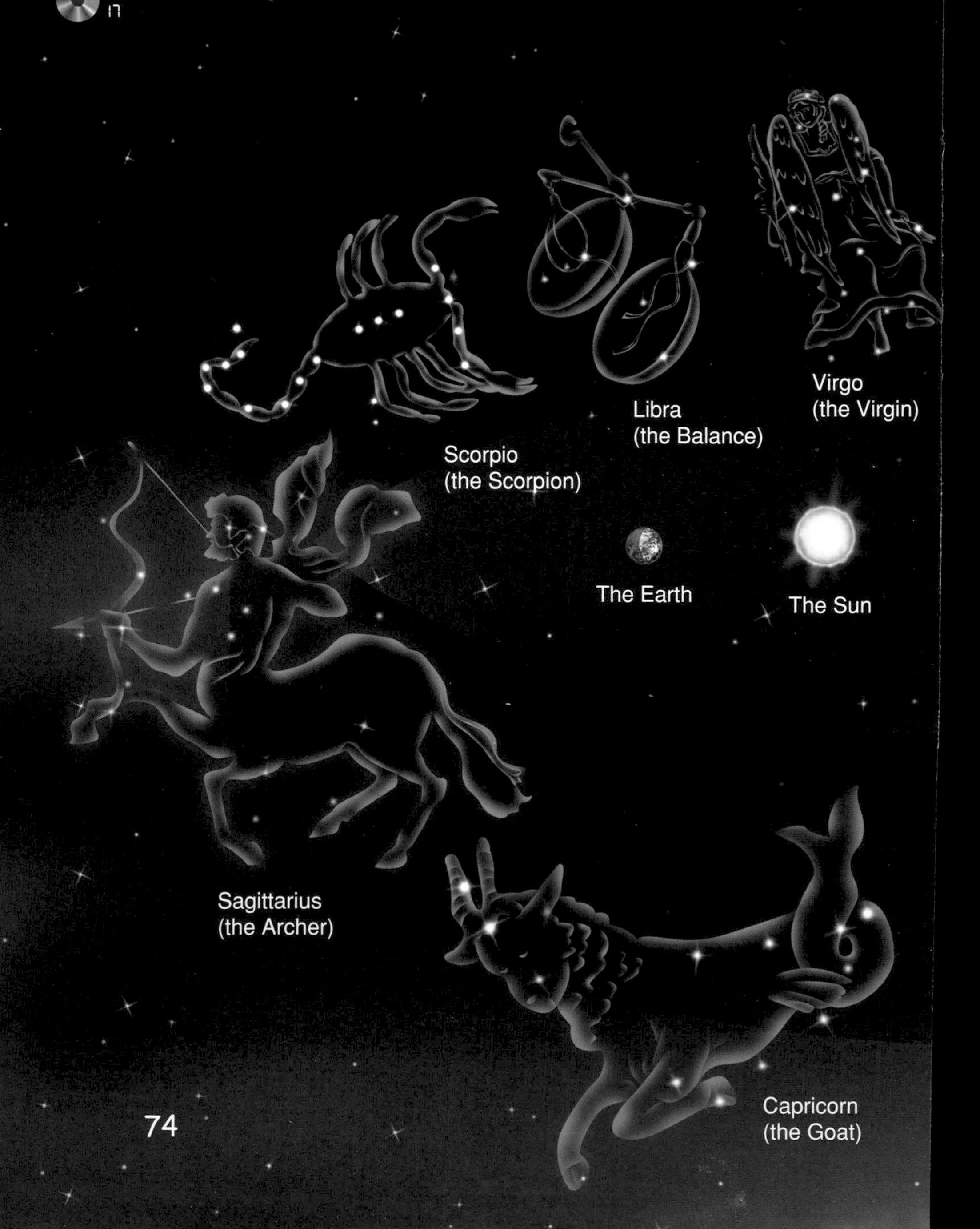

The word 'zodiac' comes from a Greek word meaning,
"the circle of animals".
Where did the zodiac come from?
In this section, you can find the Greek Myths
that explain the origins of these signs.

The Origin of the Zodiac

18

Aries (the Ram)

March 21st ~ April 20th

The origin of Aries stems from the Tale of the Golden Ram. The ram safely carried off Phrixus.
Phrixus sacrificed the Golden Ram to Zeus and in turn, Zeus placed the ram in the heavens.

Taurus (the Bull)

April 21st ~ May 20th

The origin of Taurus stems from the Tale of Europa and the Bull.
Zeus turned himself into a bull in order to attract Europa to him.
The bull carried Europa across the sea to Crete.
In remembrance, Zeus placed the image of the bull in the stars.

Gemini (the Twins)

May 21st ~ June 21st

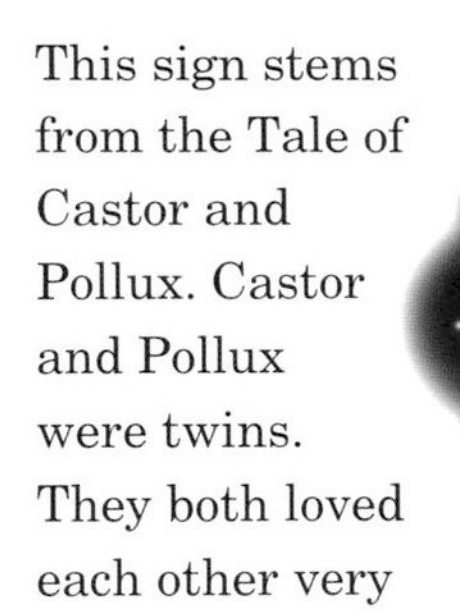

This sign stems from the Tale of Castor and Pollux. Castor and Pollux were twins.
They both loved each other very much. In honor of the brothers's great love, Zeus placed them among the stars.

19

Cancer (the Crab)

June 22nd ~ July 22nd

The sign of Cancer stems from one of the 12 Labors of Hercules.
Hera sent the crab to kill Hercules.
But Hercules crushed the crab under his foot just before he defeated the Hydra. To honor the crab, Hera placed it among the stars.

Leo (the Lion)

July 23rd ~ August 22nd

The sign of Leo stems from another of Hercules 12 Labors. Hercules's first labor was to kill a lion that lived in Nemea valley. He killed the Nemea lion with his hands.
In remembrance of the grand battle, Zeus placed the Lion of Nemea among the stars.

Virgo (the Virgin)

August 23rd ~ September 22nd

Virgo's origin stems from the Tale of Pandora. Virgo represents the goddess of purity and innocence, Astraea. After Pandora opened the forbidden box and let loose all the evils into the world, every god went back to heaven. As a remembrance of innocence lost, Astraea was placed amongst the stars in the form of Virgo.

Libra (the Balance)

September 23rd ~ October 21st

The Libra are the scales that balance justice. They are held by the goddess of divine justice, Themis. Libra shines right beside Virgo which represents Astraea, daughter of Themis.

Scorpio (the Scorpion)

October 22nd ~ November 21st

The sign of Scorpio stems from the Tale of Orion. Orion and Artemis were great hunting partners, which made Artemis's brother Apollo very jealous. Apollo pleaded with Gaea to kill Orion. So Gaea created the scorpion and killed great Orion. In remembrance of this act, Zeus placed Orion and the scorpion amongst the stars. But they never appear at the same time.

Sagittarius(the Archer)

November 23rd ~ December 21st

This sign is representative of Cheiron. Cheiron was the friend of many great heroes in Greek mythology such as Achilles and Hercules. Hercules accidentally shot Cheiron in the leg with a poison arrow. Cheiron was immortal so he couldn't die. Instead, he had to endure the unending pain. Cheiron begged Zeus to kill him. To honor Cheiron, Zeus placed him among the stars.

21

Capricorn(the Goat)

December 22nd ~ January 19th

The sign of Capricorn represents the goat Amalthea who fed the infant Zeus. It's said that Zeus placed her among the stars in gratitude.

Aquarius (the Water Bearer)

January 20th ~ February 18th

The sign of Aquarius stems from the Tale of Deucalion's Flood.
In this tale, Zeus pours all the waters of the heavens onto earth to wash away all the evil creatures. Deucalion and his wife Pyrrha were the only survivors of the great flood.

Pisces(the Fishes)

February 19th ~ March 20th

The Pisces represents the goddess of love & beauty, Aphrodite and her son the god of love, Eros. They were taking a stroll down the Euphrates River when there was a typhoon.
They pleaded for Zeus to help them escape, so Zeus changed them into fish and they swam away safely. In remembrance of this, Aphrodite is the big fish constellation and Eros is the small fish constellation.

Narcissus and Echo

卓加真　譯

歡迎來到神話的世界

神話以趣味的方式，為我們生活中的煩惱提出解釋，並滿足我們的好奇心。許多故事的編寫，都是為了解釋一些令人驚奇或恐懼的現象，因此，世界各地不同的國家、民族，都有屬於自己的神話。

希臘與羅馬神話充滿想像力，並結合了諸神與英雄們激盪人心的傳奇故事，因此特別為人所津津樂道。希臘與羅馬神話反應了真實的人類世界，因此，閱讀神話對於瞭解西方文化與思維，有極大的幫助。

這些經典故事的背景，可追溯至史前時代，但對於當代的讀者而言，它們深具魅力的法寶何在？其秘密就在於，神話能超越時空，完整地呈現人類心中的慾望。這些激盪人心的冒險故事，將帶您經歷生命中的各種重要事件：戰爭與和平、生命與死亡、善與惡，以及各種愛恨情仇。

希臘與羅馬神話裡所描繪的諸神，並不全是完美、萬能的天神，他們和人類一樣，會因憤怒而打鬥，會耍詭計戲弄其他天神，會因愛與嫉妒而感到痛苦。在 Let's Enjoy Mythology 系列的第二部 Reading Greek and Roman Mythology in English 中，你將會讀到許多具有人類特質的英雄、女英雄、眾神和女神的故事。

Reading Greek and Roman Mythology in English 將引領你穿越時空，一探想像中的古希臘世界。

前言

這本書裡講了兩則愛情悲劇：〈納西瑟斯和愛可〉和〈阿芙柔黛蒂與阿多尼斯〉。

故事一

愛可是一位美麗的山林水澤女神，而且她有一副迷人的好嗓音。不過，她有一個缺點：饒舌！有一次，宙斯和眾精靈們在玩樂，她就去和赫拉說話好讓宙斯開溜。赫拉爲此遷怒愛可，她詛咒愛可從此只能重複講出別人的話尾。

有一天，愛可遇見了美少年納西瑟斯。納西瑟斯長得很俊美，但也非常地高傲。他很無情地拒絕愛可，也傷過很多水澤女神們的心。他這麼無情，正義與復仇女神寧美息絲爲此懲罰了他，便讓他在一座泉水旁，愛上自己在水中的倒影。他愛上自己在水面上的倒影，但倒影不是眞實的，只要用手指頭一碰水面，倒影就會模糊掉。

故事二

辛勒斯國王很愛吹噓自己的女兒史麥娜，簡直可以比美美神和愛神阿芙柔黛蒂，因此觸怒了阿芙柔黛蒂，詛咒讓他的女兒史麥娜愛上自己的父王辛勒斯。史麥娜假扮成別的女子，和父親共度夜晚並生下了阿多尼斯。當父親知道了眞相之後，他氣得無法原諒女兒，想親手把她殺了。不過，阿芙柔黛蒂幫助她變成了一棵樹，而這也成了阿芙柔黛蒂和阿多尼斯的愛情故事的前曲。

現在就讓我們細細來品味他們這兩對情人的愛情故事吧！

目錄

納西瑟斯和愛可
（水仙花的由來）

p. 10

山林水澤女神，
是自然界中的美麗女性精靈，
她們整天嬉戲，歌唱。
她們不住在屋子裡，
也沒有城鎮部落，而是住在曠野裡。
住在河裡和海裡的稱為水精靈，
另外也有樹精靈和山精靈。

這是一個美麗山林女神
和一位美男子的故事。

〔圖〕山林水澤女神的生活

- **spirit** [ˋspɪrɪt]
  精靈
- **nature** [ˋneɪtʃə(r)]
  自然界
- **spend** [spend]
  花費（時間）
- **city** [ˋsɪti] 城市；都市
- **wild** [waɪld]
  曠野；野外
- **ocean** [ˋoʊʃən]
  海洋；大海
- **handsome** [ˋhænsəm]
  英俊的；俊美的

---

p. 11

愛可（迴聲）是一位迷人的山林女神，
她不僅貌美，也很有音樂天份，
她會歌唱，也會演奏各種樂器。
愛可願自己能永保純潔，
她承諾自己永遠不去戀愛。

- **most charming**
  [moust ˋtʃɑ:rmɪŋ]
  最迷人的；最有魅力的
- **musically** [ˋmju:zɪkli]
  音樂上的；音樂性的
- **talented** [ˋtæləntɪd]
  有天賦的；有才幹的
- **instrument** [ˋɪnstrəmənt]
  樂器
- **remain** [rɪˋmeɪn]
  剩下；餘留

- **pure** [pjʊr] 純潔的
- **promise herself** [`prɑ:mɪs hər`self] 承諾她自己

---

p. 12

然而，愛可有個毛病：
她太愛說話了。
有人覺得她很有趣，
有人不以爲然。
要和愛可爭辯什麼是很難的，
最後總是她辯贏。

- **however** [haʊ`evə(r)] 然而
- **fault** [fɔ:lt] 毛病
- **amusing** [ə`mju:zɪŋ] 有趣的；好玩的
- **argue** [`ɑ:rgju:] 爭辯；爭論
- **get the last word** [get ðə læst wɜ:rd] 贏得爭論；搶說最後一個字

---

p. 13

有一天，宙斯與山林精靈在嬉戲，
他常常和精靈們一起玩樂，
惹得妻子赫拉很吃醋。
突然，赫拉出現在山頂附近，
心中妒火難消。
身爲天神的宙斯，
能夠感覺得到赫拉就在附近。
他要愛可去和赫拉說話，
讓大家可以從容逃脫。

- **jealous** [`dʒeləs] 妒忌的
- **suddenly** [`sʌdənli] 意外地；冷不防地
- **appear** [ə`pɪr] 出現；顯現
- **ask** [æsk] 請求；要求
- **escape** [ə`skeɪp] 逃離；逃跑

p. 14

赫拉從山頂下來，
愛可前去向她問候。
「我的丈夫在哪？」赫拉問道。
「啊，赫拉，
婚姻與生育的女神，
妳可知道
宙斯多麼有幸能娶妳為妻呀！」
愛可的聲音非常甜美。

- **greet** [gri:t] 問候；迎接
- **marriage** [`mærɪdʒ] 婚姻
- **birth** [bɜ:rθ] 誕生；出生
- **lucky** [`lʌki] 幸運的；好運的

p. 15

「不過我沒有看到宙斯。」愛可說：
「我正巧在森林裡散步，
這裡百花盛開，
妳瞧這朵花！」
赫拉聽著愛可說話，
幾分鐘過去了，
這時間已足夠
讓宙斯和其他水澤女神離開。

- **walk in** [wɔ:k ɪn] 在……散步
- **woods** [wʊdz] 森林
- **enough** [ɪ`nʌf] 足夠的；充足的
- **get away** [get ə`weɪ] 逃脫

p. 16

然而，赫拉發現愛可在說謊，
對她大發雷霆。
「妳以為自己很聰明，」
赫拉對愛可說：「那好，
妳將無法先開口說話，
從今以後，
妳只能夠重複別人的話語，
妳這麼喜歡搶說最後一句話，
我會讓妳如願以償！
妳會全部得到的。」

- **realize** [`riəlaɪz] 領悟；了解
- **clever** [`klevə(r)] 聰明的
- **told** [toʊld] 告訴；說（tell的過去式）
- **lose** [lu:z] 失去；喪失
- **first** [fɜ:st] 第一的；首要的
- **from now on** [frəm naʊ ɑ:n] 從現在起
- **reply** [rɪ`plaɪ] 回應
- **so be it** [soʊ bi ɪt] 那麼就變成如此吧

---

p. 17

就這樣，
沒過多久，
愛可發現赫拉是如何來懲罰她的，
她現在只能重複別人說過的話，
而且只能重複那最後的幾個字。

由於再也無法表達自己的想法，
愛可非常孤單，
她變得離群索居，
自己躲在樹林深處。

- **discover** [dɪ`skʌvə(r)] 發現
- **punish** [`pʌnɪʃ] 懲罰
- **repeat** [rɪ`pi:t] 重覆
- **be only able to** 只能夠
- **few** [fju:] 很少數的
- **lonely** [`loʊnli:] 孤單的
- **more and more** 越來越多的
- **hid** [hɪd] 隱藏；藏匿（hide 的過去式）

p. 18

有位美男子，他叫做納西瑟斯，
他是河神西菲色斯
與水澤女神麗洛普的兒子。
在他誕生之時，
曾有神諭預測未來。
神諭說：「若不看到自己，
納西瑟斯將長命百歲。」
沒有人能夠完全了解其中含意，
但他的母親還是擔心，
她不允許兒子走近任何鏡子，
並拿走所有能反射的物品。
從小到大，
納西瑟斯就沒見過自己的臉。

- **name** [neɪm] 命名爲
- **oracle** [ˋɔ:rəkl] 神諭
- **future** [ˋfju:tʃə(r)] 未來
- **figure out** [ˋfɪgiər] 理解；想出
- **exactly** [ɪgˋzæktli] 正確地；精確地
- **meant** [ment] 意指；意謂（mean的過去式）
- **worried** [ˋwɜ:rid] 擔心；憂慮
- **permit** [pərˋmɪt] 允許
- **keep** [ki:p] 保持
- **shiny** [ˋʃaɪni] 發光的；閃耀的
- **thing** [θɪŋ] 事物
- **own** [oʊn] 自己的

p. 19

納西瑟斯是希臘歷史中最俊美的少年，
他的容貌，
可與阿多尼斯和戴歐尼修斯相媲美。
然而，納西瑟斯生性冷漠高傲，
許多女人和精靈愛上他，
但他一概回絕。

- **Greek** [gri:k] 希臘
- **history** [`hɪstri] 歷史
- **be compared to** [bi: kəm`peə(r)d tə] 與……相比
- **reject** [rɪ`dʒekt] 拒絕；駁回

---

p. 20

某個晴朗午後，
納西瑟斯與友人在山中狩獵，
他們看見一隻鹿，
於是開始追趕。
納西瑟斯追著追著就跌倒了，
他起身之後，卻沒看見其他友人。
他在山中上下徘徊，尋找友人。
就在此時，愛可看到了他。

- **sunny** [`sʌni] 陽光充足的；和煦的
- **run after** [rʌn `æftə(r)] 追逐的；
- **fell down** [fel daʊn] 失敗了 （fell是fall的過去式）
- **wander** [`wɑ:ndə(r)] 漫遊；閒逛
- **up and down** [ʌp ənd daʊn] 上上下下地；到處

p. 21

愛可忘了自己要保持純潔的承諾，
因爲她實在非常孤單，
而納西瑟斯是如此英俊，
愛可便愛上了他。
她跟著納西瑟斯在山中遊蕩，
悄悄躲在樹蔭下。

要是能夠先開口，
她多麼希望能夠呼喚愛人！
納西瑟斯一定會愛上她美妙的聲音的，
但因爲赫拉，
愛可根本無法先開口說話。

- **forgot** [fər`gɑ:t] 忘記（forget的過去式）
- **lonely** [`loʊnli] 孤獨的；孤單的
- **wander around** [`wɑ:ndə(r) ə`raʊnd] 到處閒逛的
- **shadow** [`ʃædoʊ] 影子

p. 22

沒多久，納西瑟斯察覺有人跟著他。
「是誰在那裡？」他喊道。
「在那裡！」愛可絕望的回應。
納西瑟斯四處張望，
沒有看到任何人。
「出來！」他說。
愛可馬上回應道：「出來！」
納西瑟斯等著，
卻沒有見到任何人。

- **after a while** [`æftə(r) ə waɪl] 過了一會兒
- **someone** [`sʌmwʌn] 某人
- **call out** [kɔ:l aʊt] 大聲喊出
- **cried** [kraɪd] 哭泣（cry的過去式）
- **desperately** [`despərətli] 絕望地；不顧一切地
- **wait** [weɪt] 等待
- **no one** [noʊ wʌn] 沒有人

p. 23

他很納悶，又說道：
「爲什麼不出來見我？」
「出來見我！」愛可回答。
「快點出來！」納西瑟斯說。
愛可又重複他的話語：
「快點出來！」

- **confused** [kən`fju:zd] 疑惑的
- **Why don't you** 你何不……？
- **let us** [let ʌs] 讓我們
- **show** [ʃoʊ] 呈現；顯示；露出

p. 24

愛可從樹後跑出來，
她想擁抱納西瑟斯，
納西瑟斯往後退，。
愛可長得很美，
但納西瑟斯太過高傲，
「把妳的手拿開！」
他咆哮著，
「我寧死也不讓妳愛我！」
「愛我！」愛可哀求著。

- **hug** [hʌg] 擁抱
- **step back** [step bæk] 往後退
- **proud** [praʊd] 驕傲的；自豪的
- **keep hands off** 把手拿開
- **shout** [ʃaʊt] 大叫；叫喊
- **rather** [`ræθər] 寧可；寧願
- **plead** [pli:d] 懇求

p. 25

但納西瑟斯的心如鐵石一般，
毫無憐憫之情，
他走開，
拋下了他不喜歡的人。

幾分鐘後，
愛可聽見他再次呼喊友人的名字，
這一次，她沒有任何回應，
她覺得很羞愧，哭著跑開。

- **have no pity for** [hæv noʊ ˋpɪti fɔ:(r)] 對……沒有同情心
- **walk away** [wɔ:k əˋweɪ] 走開
- **reply** [rɪˋplaɪ] 回應
- **ashamed** [əˋʃeɪmd] 羞愧的；感到難爲情的
- **run away** [rʌn əˋweɪ] 跑開；逃開

p. 26

〔圖〕愛可變成岩石

---

p. 27

從此之後，
其他的出林水澤女神們，
再也沒看過愛可。

愛可躲藏在洞穴和山頂，
避開和友伴有任何接觸。
她不吃也不喝。

- **never again** [ˋnevə(r) əˋgeɪn] 再也沒有；再也不曾
- **hide away** [haɪd əˋweɪ] 躲藏起來
- **mountaintop** [ˋmaʊntəntɑ:p] 山頂
- **avoid** [əˋvɔɪd] 避免；避開
- **contact** [ˋkɑ:ntækt] 接觸；碰觸

水澤女神雖然長壽，
但不是永生不死的，
她們也需要食物和水。

很快地，
愛可的身體變得愈來愈消瘦了，
她的肌肉開始萎縮，
瘦的只剩下皮包骨，
最後，她的骨頭變成了石頭，
唯一僅存的是她的聲音。

- **immortal** [ɪ`mɔ:rtl]
  不朽的；永生的
- **thinner** [`θɪnə(r)]
  更瘦的；較瘦的
- **flesh and muscle**
  [fleʃ ənd `mʌsl] 肌膚肉體
- **shrunk** [ʃrʌŋk] 萎縮
  (shrink的過去式)
- **nothing but** [`nʌθɪŋ bʌt]
  唯有；只有
- **turn into** 變成了
- **be left** [bi: left]
  被留下的
- **except** [ɪk`sept]
  除此之外；除了

---

p. 28

赫拉說過，
愛可永遠都要說最後一個字，
的確，愛可就變成了這樣子：
她的聲音迴盪山間，
深谷間都可以聽得到，
登山健行時，
就可以聽見她的聲音。

- **promise** [`prɑ:mɪs]
  承諾；諾言
- **always** [`ɔ:lweɪz] 總是
- **last** [læst] 最後的
- **hiking** [`haɪkɪŋ]
  遠足；旅行
- **twice** [twaɪs]
  兩次；兩回

你只要叫一聲，
她便會回應你，
有時甚至會重複個兩、三次。
如果你是隻身一人，
愛可的聲音可能會讓你振奮，
也可能會讓你害怕。

- **three times** [θri: taɪms] 三次
- **may** [mei] 可能也許
- **cheer . . . up** [tʃɪr ʌp] 使……高興起來
- **might** [maɪt] 可能；可以
- **scare** [sker] 驚嚇；使恐懼

---

p. 29

愛可不是唯一愛上納西瑟斯的女人，
她的許多朋友，
也對他一見鍾情，
但納西瑟斯對她們都看不上眼。
「這些女神無法吸引我，」
他心中想著：
「我是不會在她們身上浪費精神的。」

- **none** [nʌn] 一個也沒
- **attractive** [ə`træktɪv] 有吸引力的
- **waste** [weɪst] 浪費

p. 30

有一天，
一位水澤女神怨恨起了納西瑟斯。
她想，納西瑟斯太過自傲了，
她深愛著他，卻遭到無情的拒絕。
她於是對眾神禱告說：
「納西瑟斯應受到懲罰的。」
她如此禱告：
「他不懂得愛別人，
愛可因此爲他而受苦。
那麼，請讓納西瑟斯愛上他自己吧，
愛可愛他有多深，
就讓他也愛自己有多深吧，
不過，千萬別讓他如願以償。」

- **pray** [preɪ] 祈禱；祈求
- **suffer** [ˋsʌfə(r)] 受苦
- **as much as** [əz mʌtʃ əz] 如……一般多

p. 31

正義與復仇女神寧美息絲
聽見了她的禱告。
寧美息絲專門懲罰
傷愛別人的罪魁禍首，
她知道納西瑟斯對愛可無情無義，
她很同情愛可。
她也看到納西瑟斯
無情地對待精靈和少女們，
便決定應允小女神的禱告。
她會讓納西瑟斯因自己的無情與高傲，
而受到懲罰！

- **prayer** [prer] 祈禱；禱告
- **justice** [ˋdʒʌstɪs] 正義；公平；公正
- **hurt** [hɜ:rt] 傷害
- **be mean to** [bi: mi:n tə] 差勁的對待……
- **treat** [tri:t] 對待；看待
- **mean** [mi:n] 差勁的；卑劣的

---

p. 32

在納西瑟斯狩獵的山中，
隱藏著一座噴泉。
這是個美麗而神秘的仙境，
還沒有動物或人類來過附近的草地上。
這裡的水潔淨如白銀，
周圍的草地長得很高，又嫩又綠，
高大的山岩屏障著，讓陽光照不進來，
這是個與世隔絕的桃花源。

- **hidden** [ˋhɪdn] 隱藏的；隱秘的
- **spring** [sprɪŋ] 噴泉
- **secret** [ˋsi:krət] 秘密的；機密的
- **place** [pleɪs] 地方；住所
- **fresh** [freʃ] 新鮮的
- **protect** [prəˋtekt] 保護
- **ray** [reɪ] 光線

- **relaxing** [rɪˋlæksɪŋ] 令人鬆懈的；令人輕鬆的
- **magical** [ˋmædʒɪkl] 有魔力的；迷人的；神秘的

---

p. 33

這天，納西瑟斯如同往常般打獵。
他正追趕著一隻野豬，
野豬飛快奔跑，
穿過濃密的樹叢，
讓他追不上。

沒多久，納西瑟斯就在林中迷路了，
他想往回走，
但記不起來剛剛走過的路。
他從樹叢間滾落到一塊空地上，
發現了這座隱密的山泉！

- **as usual** [əz ˋjuːʒuəl] 一如往常
- **chase** [tʃeɪs] 追逐
- **boar** [bɔː(r)] 公豬；野豬
- **ran** [ræn] 跑（run的過去式）
- **through** [θruː] 穿過；越過
- **thick** [θɪk] 厚的；粗的
- **bush** [bʊʃ] 灌木；灌木叢
- **lost** [lɔːst] 迷路的
- **way** [weɪ] 路；通路；道路
- **clear** [klɪr] 空的
- **space** [speɪs] 空間

p. 34

他覺得自己很幸運，
因為他剛好口渴。
他跪下準備喝水，
突然，他第一次看到了自己的倒影，
他楞楞地看著，非常地驚訝。

納西瑟斯看到一位英俊的年輕男子，
這人有著明亮的雙眸，
他的頭髮是淡褐色的，
捲髮長得和戴歐尼修斯、阿波羅一樣；
他的雙頰豐腴紅潤，
頸項如象牙般白晰美麗；
他的紅唇微微張開，
看起來非常健美。

- **lucky** [ˋlʌki] 幸運
- **knelt down** [ˋnelt daʊn] 跪下來 （knelt 是 kneel 的過去式）
- **for the first time** [fɔ:(r) ðə fɜ:rst taɪm] 第一次
- **froze** [froʊz] 結冰；凍結（freeze的過去式）
- **in amazement** [ɪn əˋmeɪzmənt] 在驚奇中
- **bright** [braɪt] 明亮的；發亮的
- **curly** [ˋkɜ:rli] 鬈髮的
- **cheek** [tʃi:k] 臉頰；腮幫子
- **pale** [peɪl] 白晰的
- **ivory** [ˋaɪvəri] 象牙
- **perfectly** [ˋpɜ:rfɪktli:] 完美無瑕的
- **shaped** [ʃeɪpt] 成某種形狀的
- **slightly** [ˋslaɪtli] 輕微地；稍微地

p. 35

納西瑟斯看著這男子，
一見鍾情，
他從未見過如此美麗的面容。
他心想，
「這一定是某一位水精靈在看我。」
他彎下身，想親吻那張嘴唇，
但當他一碰到水面時，
那張美麗的臉卻消失了！

納西瑟斯很慌張，覺得很疑惑。
但過了一會兒，
他又見到那張美麗的臉孔，
他伸手去摸他，
結果臉孔又消失了。
但之後，臉孔又浮現出來。

- **image** [ˋɪmɪdʒ] 影像；映像
- **must** [mʌst] 必需
- **reach** [ri:tʃ] 延伸到
- **disappear** [dɪsəˋpɪə(r)] 消失
- **alarmed** [əˋlɑ:rmd] 驚恐的；受驚的
- **confused** [kənˋfju:zd] 惶惑的；困惑的

---

p. 36

他根本忘了自己很渴很餓，
就一直盯著那張臉孔，看了好久。
之後，他鼓起勇氣說：
「美麗的精靈，
你爲什麼要躲著我？

- **thirst** [θɜ:rst] 渴的
- **hunger** [ˋhʌŋgə(r)] 飢餓
- **dare** [der] 竟敢；膽敢
- **silent** [ˋsaɪlənt] 沉默的

你一定也是被我吸引住了吧，
所有的出林水澤女神都愛著我的。」
但那張臉孔只是靜默不語。

p. 37

納西瑟斯哭了起來，
他的眼淚滴入水中，
水中的臉孔開始模糊。
「請別走！」納西瑟斯哀求道，
「能讓我看著你就好，
我發誓我再也不會去碰你了。」
納西瑟斯靜止不動，
甚至連眼睛也不敢眨。
〔圖〕納西瑟斯與愛可

- **tear** [tɪr] 眼淚；淚珠
- **at least** [ət li:st] 至少
- **remain** [rɪ`meɪn] 保持；仍然
- **still** [stɪl] 還；仍舊
- **blink** [blɪŋk] 眨眼睛

p. 38

他連續幾天，
坐在那裡目不轉睛地看著水中倒影，
水中倒影也看著他。
慢慢地，
他臉上失去原有的紅潤，
身體漸漸變得虛弱。
他修長的腿，纖細的手，

- **sat** [sæt] 坐著（sit的過去式）
- **stare** [steə(r)] 盯；凝視
- **slender** [`slendə(r)] 修長的；苗條的
- **weaker** [wi:kə(r)] 更瘦弱的；更虛弱（weak弱的，weakest最弱的）

還有完美的頸項，變得愈來愈小。
他的身體愈來愈虛弱憔悴。
不久，他就沒有力氣移動身體，
只能凝視著水中的倒影。
他看到，
水中的倒影也慢慢地變化了。

---

p. 39

愛可的靈魂來到這裡看到了他。
她猜得到發生了什麼事。
她爲他感到難過，
因爲她仍深愛著他。
不過，她也幫不上忙。
當他最後要死去之前，
他輕輕地嘆了口氣，
愛可也只能重複這聲嘆息。

其他水澤女神
很快發現了納西瑟斯的遺體。
儘管納西瑟斯拒絕過她們，
她們仍舊爲他傷心落淚，
並爲他舉辦了喪禮。

- **spirit** [`spɪrɪt] 靈魂
- **guess** [ges] 猜測；推測
- **what happened** [wɑ:t `hæpənd] 發生什麼事
- **feel sorry for** [fi:l `sɑ:ri tə(r)] 爲……感到難過的
- **could do nothing for** [kəd də `nʌθɪŋ fə(r)] 對……無能爲力
- **make a sigh** [meɪk ə saɪ] 嘆了一口氣
- **repeat** [rɪ`pi:t] 重覆
- **even though** [`i:vn ðoʊ] 儘管如此
- **reject** [rɪ`dʒekt] 拒絕；駁回

- **wept over** [wept `oʊvə(r)]
  爲……哭泣；哀悼
  （wept是weep的過去式）
- **prepare . . . for . . .**
  [prɪ`per fə(r)]
  爲……準備……
- **funeral** [`fju:nərəl]
  喪葬；葬儀；出殯

---

p. 40

然而，當她們再回到這裡來時，
卻沒看到他的遺體，
只看到一朵美麗的花。
這朵花有白色的花瓣，
中間是紫色的花房。
水澤女神又驚訝又難過，
就稱這花爲「納西瑟斯」（水仙花），
以紀念他。

據說，納西瑟斯到了冥界，
仍舊看著自己的倒影。
他註定要永遠在守誓河裡，
看著自己的倒影。

- **come back** 返回；回來
- **petal** [`petl] 花瓣
- **amazed** [ə`meɪzd]
  吃驚的；顯示出驚奇的
- **look at** [lʊk ət] 注視著
- **reflection** [rɪ`flekʃn]
  倒影；映像
- **doom** [du:m]
  命中注定的；
  天數已盡的

阿芙柔黛蒂與阿多尼斯

p. 42

在塞普魯斯國，
國王叫做辛勒斯。
他育有一男一女，
女兒叫做史麥娜，
兒子叫做阿多尼斯，
但這兩個小孩並非親手足。
這是一個講阿多尼斯的生與死的故事。

- **Cyprus** 塞普魯斯
- **be named** 被命名為……
- **sister and brother** [`sɪstə(r) ənd `brʌðə(r)] 手足；兄弟姊妹

---

p. 43

在阿多尼斯出生之前，
史麥娜已經長成一位少婦了。
她美若天仙，
辛勒斯國王非常引以為傲。
國王總是這樣說：
他的女兒美若女神，
甚至還說，
女兒像女神阿芙柔黛蒂一樣美麗。
阿芙柔黛蒂長得很美，但也很善妒。
她不願自己
被拿來和凡人女子相提並論，
於是決定處罰辛勒斯國王。

- **be proud of** [bi: praʊd ʌv] 因……引以為傲
- **look like** [lʊk laɪk] 看起來像；貌似
- **as beautiful as** [əz `bju:tɪfl əz] 如……一樣美麗
- **jealous** [`dʒeləs] 妒忌
- **be compared to** [bj kəm`peə(r)d tə] 能與……相比
- **decide to** [dɪ`saɪd tə] 決定去……
- **punish** [`pʌnɪʃ] 懲罰

p. 44

阿芙柔黛蒂要兒子愛羅斯
將箭射向史麥娜。
愛羅斯的箭具有魔力，
被金箭射中的人，
會對之後所見到的第一個人一見鍾情。
阿芙柔黛蒂想讓史麥娜
愛上自己的父親，
她如此告訴兒子。

- **shoot an arrow into** [ʃu:t ən `ærou `ɪntə] 將箭射入……
- **magical** [`mædʒɪk] 有法力的
- **cause** [kɔ:z] 引起……；導致……
- **fall in love with** [fɔ:l ɪn lʌv wɪθ] 與……墜入愛河
- **happen** [`hæpən] 發生

---

p. 45

愛羅斯在一旁等待時機，
此時史麥娜正走向父親，
他便將箭射入史麥娜的心坎裡。
史麥娜是看不到這支魔箭的，
而就在她看見父親時，
她愛上了父親。

- **wait until** [weɪt ən`tɪl] 一直等到……
- **shot** [ʃɑ:t] 發射

p. 46

愛上親人當然是有悖律法，
人們認為這是罪大惡極的。
史麥娜也知道不應該，
卻無法自拔，
愛羅斯的箭是極具力量的。
史麥娜決定自殺，
但奶媽發現後制止了她，
奶媽並承諾要幫助她。

- **relative** [ˋrelətɪv] 親戚；親屬
- **against a law** [əˋgenst ə lɔ:] 違法
- **terrible** [ˋterəbl] 可怕的；嚇人的
- **too strong** [tu: strɔ:ŋ] 太強烈
- **try to** [traɪ tə] 試著去
- **kill oneself** [kɪl wʌnˋself] 自殺；自戕
- **nurse** [nɜ:rs] 褓姆；奶媽
- **promise to help** [ˋprɑ:mɪs tə help] 承諾要幫忙

---

p. 47

有一天，史麥娜的母親出城去了。
奶媽讓辛勒斯國王喝了很多酒，
她告訴國王，
有位年輕女子深愛著他。
接著，
奶媽帶著史麥娜來到父親房間。
國王喝了酒，房間裡又黑漆漆的，
根本沒有認出來那是自己的女兒。
就這樣，他們連續共度了幾個夜晚。

- **a lot of** [ə lɑ:t əv] 許多
- **truly** [ˋtru:li] 真實地；真正地
- **brought . . . to . . .** [brɔ:t tə] 為……帶來……（brought 是 bring 的過去式）
- **recognize** [ˋrekəgnaɪz] 認出
- **continue for** [kənˋtɪnju: fə(r)] 繼續去……
- **several** [ˋsevrəl] 幾個的；數個的

p. 48

一天晚上，
辛勒斯國王一時好奇，
想看看這位年輕女子的臉孔，
因此沒有喝太多酒。
史麥娜前來見他，他點起蠟燭。
當他看到自己女兒的臉孔時，
他大發雷霆。
史麥娜逃離宮殿，
而父親握著長劍一路追趕。

- **curious** [ˋkjʊriəs]
  好奇的；渴望知道
- **lit a candle**
  [lɪt ə ˋkændl]
  點燃一根蠟燭
  (lit 是 light 的過去式)
- **grab a sword**
  [græb ə sɔːrd]
  抓了一隻箭
- **chase after . . .**
  [tʃeɪs ˋæftə(r)]
  追逐……

---

p. 49

史麥娜哭著跑進森林，
她向眾神禱告讓自己消失，

阿芙柔黛蒂聽到她的禱告，
決定伸出援手。
她將史麥娜變成一棵樹，
國王辛勒斯緊追在後，
他看到女兒變成一棵樹，
仍然怒氣沖沖。

- **run into** [rʌn ˋɪntə]
  跑進去……
- **pray** [preɪ] 祈禱；祈求
- **invisible** [ɪnˋvɪzəbl]
  隱形的；看不見的
- **turn . . . into . . .**
  使變成爲……
- **right behind**
  [raɪt bɪˋhaɪnd] 就在後面
- **change into . . .** 變成……

p. 50

他拿著劍重重砍向大樹，
結果樹被從中劈成兩半，
在被劈斷的樹幹中間，
有一個嬰兒，那就是阿多尼斯，
他是國王辛勒斯
和其女兒史麥娜所生的兒子。

然而，大樹並沒有死去。
樹存活了下來，還生出許多樹苗。
許久之後，
人們會在這種樹上提煉香水。

- **split** [splɪt] 斷裂
- **in the middle of . . .** [ɪn ðə `mɪdl ʌv] 從……的中間
- **broken** [`broʊkən] 斷掉的
- **lay** [leɪ] 躺著；臥著（lie的過去式）
- **grow from . . .** 從……生長
- **seed** [si:d] 種籽
- **perfume** [`pɜ:rfju:m] 香味；芳香
- **make . . . from . . .** [meɪk frʌm] 從……製作出……

---

p. 51

國王辛勒斯看到嬰兒阿多尼斯，
想到和自己的女兒生了孩子，
眞是罪大惡極。
他再次舉起長劍，
想將阿多尼斯殺死，
但阿芙柔黛蒂從天而降，
抓起阿多尼斯，救了他。

- **raise** [reɪz] 舉起；抬起
- **come down** 降下
- **save** [seɪv] 拯救；挽救

阿芙柔黛蒂將孩子抱在胸前，
帶他來到冥后泊瑟芬住處，
她請泊瑟芬幫忙照顧小孩。

- **put in a chest**
  [pʊt ɪn ə tʃest]
  放在胸前；抱在懷裡
- **take . . . to . . .**
  帶……前往至……
- **ask . . . to . . .**
  要求……
- **take care of . . .**
  照顧……

---

p. 52

泊瑟芬專心養育孩子，
阿多尼斯漸漸長大，
長得又高又壯。
由於母親美若天仙，
阿多尼斯長得非常英俊，
冥界中的許多鬼魂，
都愛上了他。
他的俊美，也深深吸引著泊瑟芬。
但阿多尼斯不感興趣，
他不愛任何人，
直到他看見了阿芙柔黛蒂。

- **well** [wel]
  很好地；滿意地
- **grow into . . .**
  成長爲……
- **attract** [ə`trækt]
  吸引
- **be not interested**
  [bi: nɑ:t `ɪntrəstɪd]
  沒有興趣的
- **met** [mi:t]
  碰上；遇見；認識
  (meet 的過去式)

p. 53

事情是這樣發生的，
當阿芙柔黛蒂正在和愛羅斯玩耍時，
她不小心讓自己被愛羅斯的箭給插到。
她趕緊把愛羅斯推開，
但箭已經插得很深了。
然而在箭傷還未來得及痊癒之前，
她看見了阿多尼斯，
立刻墜入情網。

- **be playing with** [bi: `pleɪɪŋ wɪð] 在跟……玩耍
- **accidentally** [ˏæksɪ`dentəli] 意外地；偶然地
- **wound** [wu:nd] 傷口；創傷
- **push away** [pʊʃ ə`weɪ] 推開
- **heal** [hi:l] 治癒；痊癒

---

p. 54

她希望阿多尼斯能和她住在一起，
但泊瑟芬不願讓他走。
最後，兩位女神請宙斯來調解。
宙斯不願無端捲入爭吵，
便請謬司女神卡莉歐碧來裁決。
卡莉歐碧想盡量能兩面討好。

- **live with** [lɪv wɪθ] 與……住
- **solve** [sɑ:lv] 解決
- **get involved in** [get ɪn`vɑ:lvd ɪn] 與……牽扯在內
- **argument** [`ɑ:rgjumənt] 爭論；爭吵
- **instead** [ɪn`sted] 作爲替代
- **please** [pli:z] 使高興
- **Muse** [mju:z] 繆思女神
- **Calliope** 卡莉歐碧（司雄辯與敘事詩的女神）

p. 55

她便讓阿多尼斯與泊瑟芬
一起住四個月，
與阿芙柔黛蒂住四個月，
剩下的四個月，
他可以自己選擇伴侶。
但在每年的最後四個月裡，
阿多尼斯都選擇
和阿芙柔黛蒂一起度過。
但儘管如此，
阿芙柔黛蒂仍不滿意。
她不甘心泊瑟芬可以
和阿多尼斯共處四個月，
在一年的其他八個月時間裡，
阿芙柔黛蒂都是和阿多尼斯在一起的。

- **spend** [spend] 花費（時間）
- **one third of the year** [wʌn θɜ:rd əv ðə jɪr] 一年中的三分之一（即四個月）
- **choose** [tʃu:z] 選擇
- **partner** [ˋpɑ:rtnə(r)] 伙伴
- **be with . . .** [bi wɪð] 與……一起
- **even so** [ˋi:vn soʊ] 即使如此
- **completely** [kəmˋplitli] 完整地；完全地

---

p. 56

〔圖〕阿芙柔黛蒂與阿多尼斯
阿多尼斯年輕力壯，喜愛冒險，
熱愛狩獵野生動物。
阿芙柔黛蒂爲了和情人在一起，
甘願離開天庭。
阿多尼斯比天庭還珍貴，
她願意爲他改變生活。

- **adventurous** [ədˋventʃərəs] 愛冒險的；大膽的
- **wild animal** [waɪld ˋænɪml] 野生動物
- **heavenly** [ˋhevnli] 天國的；天堂般的
- **precious** [ˋpreʃəs]
- **lifestyle** [ˋlaɪfstaɪl] 生活方式

p. 57

在天上時，
阿芙柔黛蒂只願意待在樹蔭下，
但和阿多尼斯在一起時，
她會跟著一起去打獵。
在天上時，
阿芙柔黛蒂穿著華麗衣裳，
但和阿多尼斯在一起時，
她會換上獵裝。
阿芙柔黛蒂不喜歡戶外活動，
但為了阿多尼斯，
她在山間奔跑，在樹林間穿梭。
她是美麗女神，
但當她和阿多尼斯在一起時，
卻倒像是狩獵女神阿蒂蜜絲。

- **would** [wʊd]
  願意；要
- **in the shade** [ɪn ðə ʃeɪd]
  蔭；陰涼處
- **hunting clothes**
  [`hʌntɪŋ kloʊz]
  獵裝
- **the outdoors**
  [ðə `aʊt`dɔ:rz]
  戶外
- **through** [θru:]
  穿過；越過
- **Artemis**阿蒂蜜絲
  （狩獵女神）

---

p. 58

阿芙柔黛蒂的膽子不大，
只敢和阿多尼斯一起獵兔子和小鹿。
她告誡阿多尼斯小心凶猛動物，
要他不要去獵獅子或野豬。
「對容易受驚的動物，
可以放膽去追逐。」

- **bold** [boʊld]
  英勇的；無畏的
- **warn** [wɔ:rn]
  警告；告誡
- **dangerous** [`deɪndʒərəs]
  危險的

她告訴阿多尼斯。
「但狩獵凶猛動物是很危險的，
千萬要小心，
別攻擊那些生性兇猛的動物，
不要讓自己受到危險，
不要讓我們的幸福遭受威脅！」
阿芙柔黛蒂說。

- **boar** [bɔ:r] 公豬
- **brave** [breɪv] 英勇的；勇敢的
- **shy** [ʃaɪ] 膽小的；易受驚的
- **fierce** [fɪrs] 兇猛的；好鬥的
- **beast** [bi:st] 野獸
- **nature** [`neɪtʃə] 自然界
- **attack** [ə`tæk] 攻擊

---

p. 59

「我愛你之深，
你無需以勇氣證明，
你的美貌不會使獅子或野豬動心，
想想牠們的利爪和尖牙，
我眞討厭這些動物！」
阿芙柔黛蒂說完話，
便轉身準備離去。
她和塞普魯斯有約，
於是她坐上天鵝座車，馭風而去。

- **prove** [pru:v] 證明
- **bravery** [`breɪvəri] 勇氣
- **impress** [ɪm`pres] 感動
- **claw** [klɔ:] 爪子
- **warn** [wɔ:rn] 警告；告誡
- **prepare to . . .** 準備去……
- **have an appointment** [həv ən ə`pɔɪntmənt] 有個會面
- **got into** [gɑ:t `ɪntə] 使穿上；此指坐上
- **chariot** [`tʃæriət] 馬車；戰車
- **swan** [swɑ:n] 天鵝
- **drove away** [droʊv ə`weɪ] 駛離（drove 是 drive 的過去式）
- **the air** [ði er] 天空；大氣

p. 60

但是阿多尼斯心高氣傲，
沒有理會阿芙柔黛蒂的忠告，
他可不是個膽小柔弱的男孩，
他可是身強力壯的。
因此當獵犬在樹叢中發現野豬時，
阿多尼斯隨即緊追在後。
他擲出長矛，刺進野豬體內。
但野豬傷得不重，
牠用嘴巴就將長矛拉出。

- **too pround to . . .** [tu: praʊd tə] 太自豪而不去……
- **advice** [əd`vaɪs] 建議
- **scared** [skerd] 恐懼的；害怕的
- **in the bushes** [ɪn ðə `bʊʃɪs] 在灌木叢中
- **chase after** [tʃeɪs `æftə(r)] 追趕……
- **threw** [θru:] 扔；擲（throw 的過去式）
- **spear** [spɪr] 矛
- **stuck** [stʌk] 刺（stick 的過去式）
- **serious** [`sɪriəs] 嚴重的
- **pull out** [pʊl aʊt] 拔出

---

p. 61

有人說這隻野豬是戰神阿瑞士，
他也是阿芙柔黛蒂的情人，
阿多尼斯和泊瑟芬在一起時，
阿芙柔黛蒂便和阿瑞士在一起，
阿瑞士對阿多尼斯很嫉妒。
這一天，他將自己變成一隻野豬，
如此一來，
便可以偷偷把阿多尼斯幹掉。

- **Ares**阿瑞士
- **secretly** [`si:krətlɪ] 秘密地；背地裡

野豬衝向阿多尼斯，
阿多尼斯奮力逃命，
但很少人能夠逃得過野豬的追逐。
這隻動物追上阿多尼斯，把他撞倒，
將長牙一舉深深刺入阿多尼斯的肚腹。

- **caught up** [kɔ:t ʌp]
  趕上
  （caught是catch的過去式）
- **knock over**
  [nɑ:k `oʊvə(r)] 撞倒
- **bury . . . into**
  [`beri `ɪntə]
  將……埋入……
  （buried是bury的過去式）
- **tusk** [tʌsk] 長牙
- **stomach** [`stʌmək] 胃部

---

p. 62

阿多尼斯躺在草地上，
奄奄一息。
最後，獵犬將野豬驅離，
但一切爲時已晚。
阿多尼斯大聲哀號著。

阿芙柔黛蒂聽到淒厲的哀號聲，
便將天鵝座車轉向，
火速趕回來。
〔圖〕阿多尼斯之死

- **on the grass**
  [ɑ:n ðə græs] 在草地上
- **moan out** [moʊn aʊt]
  大聲哀號
- **loud** [laʊd] 大聲的
- **rush back** [rʌʃ bæk]
  倉促地返回

p. 63

阿芙柔黛蒂靠近一看，
只見眼前恐怖的景象。
她的情郎已臥倒在血泊之中！
她從座車跳下來，
直奔向阿多尼斯。
她淚水奪眶而出，
捶胸頓足，悔恨不已。
既使她是女神，
也無法救治阿多尼斯。

- **sight** [saɪt] 景象
- **laying in the ground** [leɪŋ ɪn ðə groʊnd] 躺在地上
- **be covered in blood** [bi: `kʌvərd ɪn blʌd] 被血跡沾滿
- **hit her own chest** [hɪt hə(r) oʊn tʃest] 搥打她自己的胸口
- **in frustration** [ɪn frʌ`streɪʃən] 在挫折中

---

p. 64

她拉扯頭髮，對天哀號。
「啊，可悲的命運，
爲何對我如此殘忍？」
但命運將無法得勝，
我悲傷的記憶將永不被遺忘，
它每年都將重複一次，
我的愛人，阿多尼斯，
你的血將化爲花朵，
這朵花每年都會綻放，
讓人們記得我對你的愛。」

- **grab hair and pull** [græb her ənd pʊl] 拉扯頭髮
- **shout** [ʃaʊt] 大叫；呼喊
- **fate** [feɪt] 命運
- **treat** [tri:t] 對待
- **memory** [`meməri] 記憶
- **grief** [gri:f] 悲痛；悲傷
- **bloom** [blu:m] 綻放；盛開
- **remind** [rɪ`maɪnd] 提醒

p. 65

說完，阿芙柔黛蒂將幾滴瓊汁玉液
倒在阿多尼斯的血液上。
兩者一混和，
馬上產生泡沫。

一個鐘頭過後，
竟神奇地長出了一朵花。
花是緋紅色的，
一如阿多尼斯的鮮血；
花綻放的時間極短，
風一來，花便綻放，
但花瓣會隨即隨風而落。

正因如此，
這種花就叫做「風之花」
或「秋牡丹」。
風讓花兒綻放，
也將花兒摧毀。

- **pour** [pɔ:(r)] 灌；倒
- **some drops of . . .** [səm drɑ:ps ʌv] 幾滴……
- **nectar** [ˋnektə(r)] 瓊漿玉液
- **mix** [mɪks] 混和
- **bubble** [ˋbʌbl] 泡泡；泡沫
- **magically** [ˋmædʒɪklɪ] 有魔法地；不可思議地
- **blow** [blo] 吹；刮
- **Anemone**秋牡丹
- **destroy** [dɪˋstrɔɪ] 毀壞

閱讀測驗

閱讀下列問題並選出最適當的答案。 ➜ 66-73 頁

▲納西瑟斯和愛可

1. 爲什麼赫拉會對愛可生氣？
   (A) 因爲愛可是宙斯的愛人。
   (B) 因爲愛可對赫拉說謊。
   (C) 因爲愛可不想談戀愛。
   (D) 因爲赫拉忌妒愛可的聲音。

答案 (B)

2. 赫拉對愛可做了什麼？
   (A) 她讓愛可消失不見了。
   (B) 她讓愛可失去先開口說話的能力。
   (C) 她讓愛可談戀愛了。
   (D) 她把愛可變成一頭野豬。

答案 (B)

3. 神諭說納西瑟斯會發生什麼事？
   (A) 他會成爲希臘最英俊的男人。
   (B) 他無法愛任何人。
   (C) 如果他不看見自己，就能長壽。
   (D) 他一生都在打獵。

答案 (C)

4. 為什麼有那麼多女人和精靈愛上了納西瑟斯？

(A) 因為他既年輕又勇敢。

(B) 因為他唱歌很好聽。

(C) 因為他非常英俊。

(D) 因為他很自傲。

答案 (C)

5. 納西瑟斯如何看待愛上他的女人？

(A) 他誰都不喜歡。

(B) 他對她們都感到害怕。

(C) 他每個都喜歡。

(D) 他不相信她們任何一個人

答案 (A)

6. 納西瑟斯在狩獵什麼動物的時候迷路了？

(A) 一隻鹿。

(B) 一隻兔子。

(C) 一頭熊。

(D) 一隻野豬。

答案 (C)

7. 當納西瑟斯從樹叢間摔落時，他發現了什麼？

(A) 一面鏡子。

(B) 一顆閃耀的石頭。

(C) 一處隱密的泉水地。

(D) 愛可。

答案 (C)

8. 納西瑟斯覺得他自己的倒影是什麼？

(A) 他自己。

(B) 一位水精靈。

(C) 一位天神。

(D) 一個水澤女神。

答案 (B)

9. 當水澤女神返回到納西瑟斯的遺體旁時，她們看到了什麼？

(A) 一朵花。

(B) 只看到草地。

(C) 血跡。

(D) 骨頭。

答案 (A)

10. 是哪一位天神懲罰納西瑟斯的？

答案 Nemesis 寧美息絲。

▲阿芙柔黛蒂與阿多尼斯

1. 史麥娜是阿多尼斯的什麼人？

(A) 姐姐。

(B) 母親。

(C) 阿姨。

(D) 奶媽。

答案 (B)

2. 阿芙柔黛蒂是怎麼懲罰辛勒斯的？

(A) 她讓史麥娜殺了辛勒斯。

(B) 她讓愛羅斯將愛神的箭射到辛勒斯身上。

(C) 她讓史麥娜愛上父親辛勒斯。

(D) 她派戰神阿瑞士殺了辛勒斯。

答案 (C)

3. 阿多尼斯是如何出生的？

(A) 一棵樹被劈成兩半後出生的。

(B) 從他父親的思想中誕生出來的。

(C) 自然生產的。

(D) 一個野生動物生的。

答案 (A)

4. 誰從阿多尼斯的父親手中救回阿多尼斯的？

(A) 泊瑟芬。

(B) 史麥娜。

(C) 大自然。

(D) 阿芙柔黛蒂。

答案 (D)

5. 阿多尼斯是在哪裡長大的？

(A) 在父親的皇宮裡。

(B) 在洞穴裡。

(C) 在冥界。

(D) 在阿芙柔黛蒂的家。

答案 (C)

6. 爲什麼阿芙柔黛蒂會愛上阿多尼斯？

(A) 她被兒子愛神的神奇之箭所傷。

(B) 她喝錯了神奇藥水。

(C) 她看上了阿多尼斯的美貌。

(D) 她忌妒泊瑟芬。

答案 (A)

7. 阿多尼斯一年中花多少時間與泊瑟芬在一起？

(A) 二分之一年。

(B) 三分之二年。

(C) 四個月。

(D) 三個月。

答案 (C)

8. 阿瑞士對阿多尼斯是什麼觀感？

(A) 欽佩。

(B) 忌妒。

(C) 愛意。

(D) 害怕。

答案 (B)

9. 阿多尼斯是怎麼死的？

(A) 他落在他自己的矛上。

(B) 他自己的狗攻擊他。

(C) 一頭野豬殺了他。

(D) 他從阿芙柔黛蒂的馬車上摔下。

答案 (C)

10. 阿多尼斯是怎麼變成一朵花的？

答案 Aphrodite poured some drops of nectar on Adonis s blood. After about an hour, a flower magically grew up in the bubbles of the mixture.

阿芙柔黛蒂將幾滴瓊汁玉液倒在阿多尼斯的血液上，兩者一混和，馬上產生泡沫。

※閱讀下段文章，並討論之以下的問題。

……有一天，一位水澤女神怨恨起了納西瑟斯。
她想，納西瑟斯太過自傲了，
她深愛著他，卻遭到無情的拒絕。
她於是對眾神禱告說：「納西瑟斯應受到懲罰的。」
她如此禱告：「他不懂得愛別人，
愛可因此為他而受苦。
那麼，請讓納西瑟斯愛上他自己吧，
愛可愛他有多深，就讓他也愛自己有多深吧，
不過，千萬別讓他如願以償。」……

1. 如果你是水澤女神，你會想要納西瑟斯怎麼被懲罰？

參考答案

I would want Narcissus to fall in love with a woman who would reject him.

我會希望納西瑟斯愛上一個會拒絕他的女人。

……她希望阿多尼斯能和她住在一起，

但泊瑟芬不願讓他走。

最後，兩位女神請宙斯來調解。宙斯不願無端捲入爭吵，便請謬司女神卡莉歐碧來裁決。

卡莉歐碧想盡量能兩面討好。

她便讓阿多尼斯與泊瑟芬一起住四個月，與阿芙柔黛蒂住四個月，剩下的四個月，他可以自己選擇伴侶。

但在每年的最後四個月裡，

阿多尼斯都選擇和阿芙柔黛蒂一起度過。……

2. 如果你是卡莉歐碧，你會怎麼決定？

參考答案

I would want ask Adonis to choose which goddess he wanted to stay with.

我會要阿多尼斯自己選擇他想跟哪位女神在一起。

黃道十二宮

黃道十二宮 ➜ 64~68 頁

「黃道帶」(zodiac)這個字源自希臘文，意指「動物的環狀軌道」。黃道帶的起源爲何？在本篇裡，你將可以看到說明星座來源的希臘神話故事：

太陽(the Sun)、地球(the Earth)、牡羊座(the Ram)、金牛座(the Bull)、雙子座(the Twins)、巨蟹座(the Crab)、獅子座(the Lion)、處女座(the Virgin)、天秤座(the Balance)、天蠍座(the Scorpion)、射手座(the Archer)、摩羯座(the Goat)、寶瓶座(the Water Bearer)、雙魚座(the Fishes)。

1. Aries (the Ram) 牡羊座
2. Libra (the Balance) 天秤座
3. Taurus (the Bull) 金牛座
4. Scorpio (the Scorpion) 天蠍座
5. Gemini (the Twins) 雙子座
6. Sagittarius (the Archer) 射手座
7. Cancer (the Crab) 巨蟹座
8. Capricorn (the Goat) 摩羯座
9. Leo (The Lion) 獅子座
10. Aquarius (the Water Bearer) 寶瓶座
11. Virgo (the Virgin) 處女座
12. Pisces (the Fishes) 雙魚座

牡羊座（the Ram） 3.21-4.20

牡羊座源自於金羊毛的故事。白羊安全營救福里瑟斯，福里瑟斯把金羊獻祭給宙斯作爲回報，宙斯便將金羊形象化爲天上星座。

金牛座（the Bull） 4.21-5.20

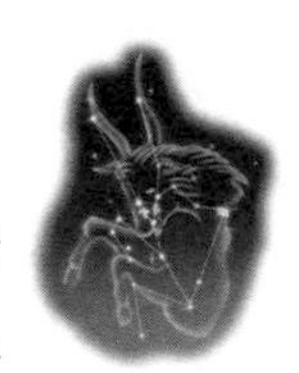

金牛座源自於歐羅巴和公牛的故事。宙斯化身爲公牛，以便吸引歐羅巴，公牛載著歐羅巴跨海來到克里特島。宙斯將公牛的形象化爲星座，以爲紀念。

雙子座（the Twins） 5.21-6.21

雙子座源自於卡斯特與波樂克斯的故事。他們兩人爲攣生兄弟，彼此相親相愛。爲了紀念其兄弟情誼，宙斯將他們的形象化爲星座。

巨蟹座（the Crab） 6.22-7.22

巨蟹座源自於赫丘力的十二項苦差役。希拉派遣巨蟹前去殺害赫丘力，但是赫丘力在打敗九頭蛇之前，一腳將巨蟹踩碎。爲了紀念巨蟹，希拉將其形象化爲星座。

獅子座（The Lion） 7.23-8.22

獅子座亦源自於赫丘力十二項苦差中。赫丘力的第一項苦差，是要殺死奈米亞山谷之獅。他徒手殺了獅子，爲了紀念這項偉大的事蹟，宙斯將奈米亞獅子的形象，置於星辰之中。

處女座（the Virgin） 8.23-9.22

處女座源自於潘朵拉的故事。處女指的是純潔與天眞女神阿絲蒂雅。潘朵拉好奇將禁盒打開，讓許多邪惡事物來到人間，眾神紛紛返回天庭。爲了紀念這種失落的純眞，便把阿絲蒂雅的形象置於群星中。

天秤座（the Balance） 9.23-10.21

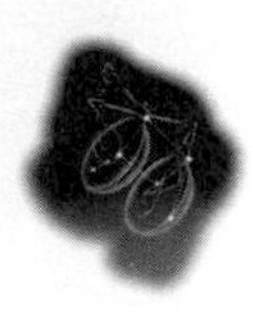

天秤是正義的秤子，由神聖正義女神蒂米絲隨身攜帶。天秤座落在處女座旁邊，因為阿絲蒂雅是蒂米絲之女。

天蠍座（the Scorpion） 10.22-11.21

天蠍座源自於歐里昂。歐里昂和阿蒂蜜絲是一對狩獵夥伴，阿蒂蜜絲的哥哥阿波羅對此忌妒不已。他請求蓋亞殺了歐里昂。因此，蓋亞創造天蠍殺了偉大的歐里昂。為了紀念此事，宙斯將歐里昂和天蠍化成星座。這兩個星座從來不會同時出現。

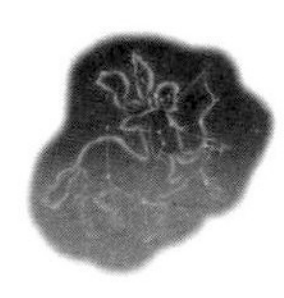

射手座（the Archer） 11.23-12.21

射手座代表卡隆。在希臘神話故事中，卡隆是許多英雄的朋友，例如亞吉力、赫丘力。赫丘力以毒箭誤傷了卡隆。卡隆是神，因此得以不死，但是卻必須忍受這無止盡的痛苦，所以卡隆央求宙斯殺了他。為了紀念卡隆，宙斯將他化為星座。

摩羯座（the Goat） 12.22-1.19

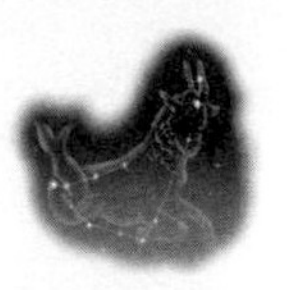

魔羯代表哺育年幼宙斯的羊阿瑪爾夏。
據說宙斯爲了感念此羊，將之化爲星座。

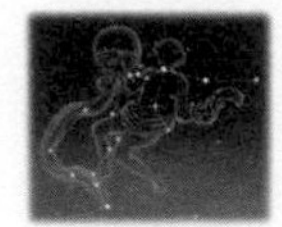

寶瓶座（the Water Bearer） 1.20-2.18

寶瓶座源自於鐸卡連的洪水。在這個故事中，宙斯在人間降下豪雨，讓洪水沖走一切邪惡的生物。只有鐸卡連和妻子皮雅是洪水的生還者。

雙魚座（the Fishes） 2.19-3.20

雙魚座代表愛與美之女神阿芙柔黛蒂，以及其子愛神愛羅斯。當時有個颱風，兩人沿著優芙瑞特河步行。他們請求宙斯援救，宙斯將兩人變成魚，讓他們安然渡過風災。爲了紀念此事，阿芙柔黛蒂化身爲星座中的大魚，愛羅斯則化爲小魚。

Without a knowledge of mythology much of the elegant literature of our own language cannot be understood and appreciated.

缺少了神話知識，就無法了解和透徹語言的文學之美。

—Thomas Bulfinch

Thomas Bulfinch（1796-1867），出生於美國麻薩諸塞州的Newton，隨後全家移居波士頓，父親爲知名的建築師Charles Bulfinch。他在求學時期，曾就讀過一些優異的名校，並於1814年畢業於哈佛。

畢業後，執過教鞭，爾後從商，但經濟狀況一直未能穩定。1837年，在銀行擔任一般職員，以此爲終身職業。後來開始進一步鑽研古典文學，成爲業餘作家，一生未婚。

1855年，時值59歲，出版了奠立其作家地位的名作*The Age of Fables*，書中蒐集希臘羅馬神話，廣受歡迎。此書後來與日後出版的 *The Age of Chivalry*（1858）和 *Legends of Charlemagne*（1863），合集更名爲 *Bulfinch's Mythology*。

本系列書系，即改編自 *The Age of Fable*。Bulfinch 著寫本書時，特地以成年大眾爲對象，以將古典文學引介給一般大眾。*The Age of Fable* 堪稱十九世紀的羅馬神話故事的重要代表著作，其中有很多故事來源，來自Bulfinch自己對奧維德（Ovid）的《變形記》（*Metamorphoses*）的翻譯。

■Bulfinch 的著作

1. Hebrew Lyrical History.
2. The Age of Fable: Or Stories of Gods and Heroes.
3. The Age of Chivalry.
4. The Boy Inventor: A Memoir of Matthew Edwards, Mathematical-Instrument Maker.
5. Legends of Charlemagne.
6. Poetry of the Age of Fable.
7. Shakespeare Adapted for Reading Classes.
8. Oregon and Eldorado.
9. Bulfinch's Mythology: Age of Fable, Age of Chivalry, Legends of Charlemagne.